HUNTED BY THE INSECT ARMY

DINOSAUR COVE™

DINOSAUR COVE™

HUNTED BY THE INSECT ARMY

by
REX STONE

illustrated by
MIKE SPOOR

Series created by
Working Partners Ltd

OXFORD
UNIVERSITY PRESS

For Maggie   R.S.

Dedicated to Harriet with thanks for her design expertise   M.S.

OXFORD
UNIVERSITY PRESS

Great Clarendon Street, Oxford OX2 6DP
Oxford University Press is a department of the University of Oxford.
It furthers the University's objective of excellence in research, scholarship,
and education by publishing worldwide in

Oxford   New York

Auckland   Cape Town   Dar es Salaam   Hong Kong   Karachi
Kuala Lumpur   Madrid   Melbourne   Mexico City   Nairobi

British Library Cataloguing in Publication Data

Data available

ISBN: 978-0-19-275633-6

1 3 5 7 9 10 8 6 4 2

Printed in Great Britain
Paper used in the production of this book is a natural,
recyclable product made from wood grown in sustainable forests
The manufacturing process conforms to the environmental
regulations of the country of origin

FACT FILE

➡ JAMIE AND TOM HAVE DISCOVERED THE SECRET OF DINOSAUR COVE. WHEN THEY STEP THROUGH A SET OF FOSSILIZED PRINTS, THEY'RE MAGICALLY TRANSPORTED TO DINO WORLD! THE BOYS DECIDE TO VISIT THE PERMIAN ERA, A TIME SO LONG AGO THAT DINOSAURS DON'T EXIST YET. THE HOT FORESTS ARE SWARMING WITH GIANT INSECTS. BUT THE PERMIAN ERA IS ABOUT TO END...WILL THE BOYS GET HOME SAFELY? OR WILL THEY BECOME EXTINCT?

JAMIE

- FULL NAME: JAMIE MORGAN
- AGE: 8 YEARS
- SIZE: 1 JATOM*
- TOP SPEED: 10 KPH
- LIKES: FOSSIL HUNTING AND LEARNING ABOUT DINOSAURS
- DISLIKES: BEING STUCK INDOORS

Jamie's eye

Jamie's foot

Jamie's hand

*NOTE A JATOM IS THE SIZE OF JAMIE OR TOM: 125 CM TALL AND 27 KG IN WEIGHT

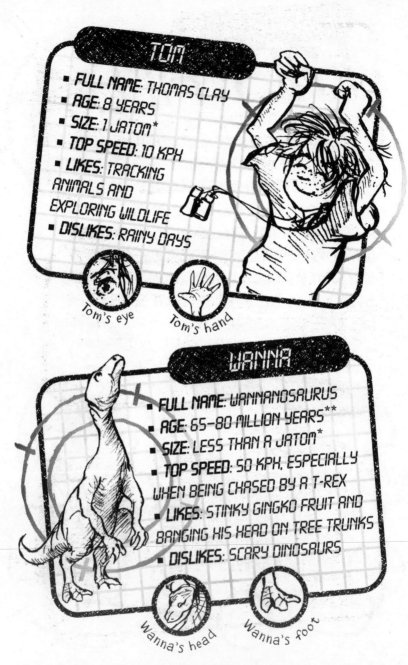

TOM

- **FULL NAME:** THOMAS CLAY
- **AGE:** 8 YEARS
- **SIZE:** 1 JATOM*
- **TOP SPEED:** 10 KPH
- **LIKES:** TRACKING ANIMALS AND EXPLORING WILDLIFE
- **DISLIKES:** RAINY DAYS

Tom's eye

Tom's hand

WANNA

- **FULL NAME:** WANNANOSAURUS
- **AGE:** 65–80 MILLION YEARS**
- **SIZE:** LESS THAN A JATOM*
- **TOP SPEED:** 50 KPH, ESPECIALLY WHEN BEING CHASED BY A T-REX
- **LIKES:** STINKY GINGKO FRUIT AND BANGING HIS HEAD ON TREE TRUNKS
- **DISLIKES:** SCARY DINOSAURS

Wanna's head

Wanna's foot

*NOTE: A JATOM IS THE SIZE OF JAMIE OR TOM: 125 CM TALL AND 27 KG IN WEIGHT
**NOTE: SCIENTISTS CALL THIS PERIOD THE LATE CRETACEOUS

APTHOROBLATTINA

- **FULL NAME:** APTHOROBLATTINA
- **AGE:** 250 MILLION YEARS***
- **LENGTH:** AT LEAST 5 TIMES BIGGER THAN A COCKROACH TODAY
- **LIKES:** WORKING IN A TEAM
- **DISLIKES:** SHARING FOOD

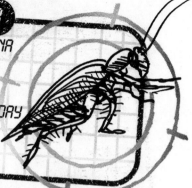

ODONATA

- **FULL NAME:** ODONATA
- **AGE:** 250 MILLION YEARS***
- **WEIGHT:** ONE FIFTH OF A JATOM*
- **LENGTH:** HALF A JATOM*
- **LIKES:** FLYING VERY FAST
- **DISLIKES:** OTHER POND CREATURES

PERMARACHNE

- **FULL NAME:** PERMARACHNE
- **AGE:** 250 MILLION YEARS***
- **WEIGHT:** ONE THIRD OF A JATOM*
- **LENGTH:** HALF A JATOM*
- **LIKES:** TRAPPING FOOD IN ITS WEB
- **DISLIKES:** ITS LAIR BEING INVADED

*NOTE: A JATOM IS THE SIZE OF JAMIE OR TOM: 125 CM TALL AND 27 KG IN WEIGHT
***NOTE: SCIENTISTS CALL THIS PERIOD THE PERMIAN

DINOSAUR COVE

Village

Marina

Sealight Head

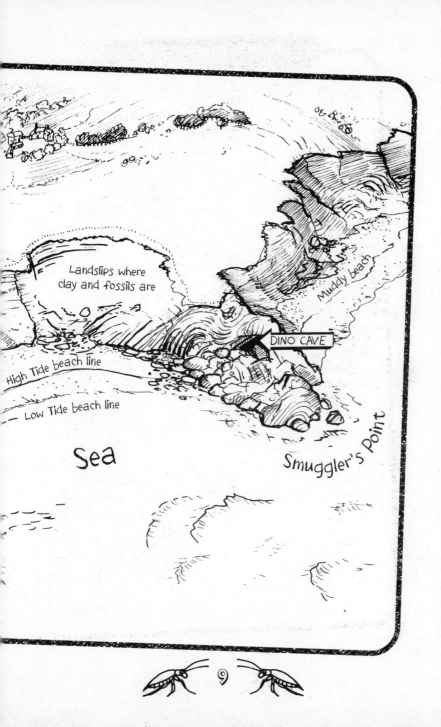

Landslips where
clay and fossils are

DINO CAVE

Muddy beach

High Tide beach line

Low Tide beach line

Sea

Smuggler's Point

CHAPTER 1

Tom Clay ran into the garden of the old
Dinosaur Cove lighthouse and stopped dead.

'What are you up to, Jamie?' he asked.

His best friend, Jamie Morgan, was
standing on a bed sheet and poking a rake
into the branches of the tree above his head.

'You're just in time,' he said, grinning.
'Grandad told me to try this. He said I'd see
something amazing.'

'Go for it!' said Tom, joining him.

Jamie gave the branches a good rattle.

'Whoa!' he cried, jumping back in surprise as a shower of tiny insects fell from the tree. 'It's raining bugs!' Tom gasped.

Jamie dropped to his knees to inspect the wriggling creatures on the sheet. He picked up the magnifying glass that lay ready next to it.

'Awesome,' he exclaimed, as they peered through it together. 'Grandad was right—this is amazing.'

'Beetles, ants, woodlice,' Tom pointed out, 'and look at that hairy caterpillar. Hey, my mum wouldn't like those spiders!'

Jamie held the magnifying glass over a small black beetle. The boys could see every detail of its hard, shiny back and waving antennae.

'Scary!' exclaimed Jamie. 'I've turned it into an armoured monster!'

'That armour's its exoskeleton,' Tom told him. 'Insects have their skeletons on the outside. And check out those jaws.'

Jamie's eyes lit up. 'I know where we can see some giant insects for real.'

'Dino World!' declared Tom. 'We just need your Fossil Finder and the Permian trilobite.'

'Got them here!' cried Jamie, patting the backpack that went everywhere with him. He slipped the magnifying glass inside and they were ready to go.

Dino World was the boys' amazing secret. One day, while exploring the old smugglers' cave in the cliffs, they'd discovered a hidden chamber. At the back was the entrance to a land of living dinosaurs. All they needed was a prehistoric fossil to open the way to adventure.

They sprinted down the craggy lighthouse steps, sped across the beach, and climbed up to the dark, deserted cave. They dropped to their hands and knees and squeezed through the hidden opening. Tom shone his torch over the line of fossilized dinosaur prints that led to the sheer rock wall.

'Ready?' Jamie felt himself fizzing with excitement as he placed his feet in the first two prints.

'Right behind you!' said Tom. 'One . . . two . . . '

Jamie took up the count. 'Three . . . four . . . five!'

There was a blinding flash, the rock wall vanished, and the boys found themselves in the familiar underground cave at the base of the towering Permian volcano.

'It's hotter than ever,' said Tom, wiping his forehead.

Jamie wrinkled his nose. 'And something smells like rotten eggs!'

'It's just like that stink bomb my brother made,' said Tom.

As the boys climbed upwards towards the light, a heavy black cloud passed overhead. It blocked out the sun for a moment.

'Is it going to rain?' Jamie wondered.

'That cloud looked more like smoke,' answered Tom, hauling himself up to the opening.

Cautiously, they poked their heads out.

WHOOOSH!

They whipped round. About a T-Rex length away, a fountain of red lava was shooting into the air and falling in a seething puddle. It bubbled in a thin stream down the mountain slope, away from the cave opening.

'What's happening?' gasped Jamie. 'Is the volcano erupting?'

'I don't think so,' said Tom, as they scrambled up into the scorching heat. 'But check out the plain. We've never seen it like that before!'

HISSSS!

Loud eruptions
of smoking lava were
shooting up from cracks
all over the hard-baked
earth. Black smoke
billowed into the air.

Tom looked at Jamie,
eyes wide. 'Something big's
going on here,' he said.

'Then we need to find
out what it is,' declared
Jamie.

Jamie whipped his Fossil Finder out of the backpack. **'HAPPY HUNTING'** appeared on the screen of the hand-held computer. 'I'm going to search for clues. Permian lava . . . bad smell . . . ' He tapped the keywords in, pressed **'ENTER'**—and nearly dropped the Fossil Finder in shock. 'Mass Extinction! The Permian age is coming to an end.'

Tom read over his friend's shoulder. 'It was caused by rising temperatures. That eggy smell is hydrogen sulphide heating up deep under

the sea and bubbling to the surface.
Ninety-five per cent of all life on
Earth is going to die—including insects!'

'Then we can't stay for long,' said Jamie,
slipping the Fossil Finder into his backpack.
'We'd better take a quick look at those giant
bugs and get out of here.'

'Wait a minute,' said Tom suddenly. He
pointed to the red sand outside the tunnel. There
was a trail of footprints embedded in it. 'They
look like Wanna's prints! But where is he?'

Wanna was a little wannanosaurus who
always turned up when the boys visited Dino
World, and they'd never been exploring
without him. The friendly Cretaceous

SSS

dinosaur was usually waiting to cover
them in raspy licks. But today he was
nowhere to be seen.

'We've got to find him,' said Jamie,
scanning the angry plain ahead and the
rugged volcano slopes behind. 'Or he'll end
up extinct too!'

'Let's check round the gingko trees first,'
Tom said. 'He's probably enjoying a snack of
his favourite fruit.'

The boys set off across the plain, heading
for the forest. A blast of scalding steam
suddenly hissed up at their feet. They jumped
aside just in time.

'Steer clear of the cracks,' called Tom. 'We don't want to be boiled alive.'

'And keep an eye out for the inostrancevia,' warned Jamie. He glanced around for the fierce, bear-like predator that seemed to appear whenever the boys visited the Permian. 'Coast's clear!' he said. 'In fact, there's nothing moving at all.'

'The changes to the climate must be upsetting the wildlife,' said Tom.

They left the plain with its shooting geysers and walked into the welcome shade of the forest.

Grunk!

'Did you hear that?' asked Jamie.

GRUNK! GRUNK!

'That's Wanna.' Tom broke into a run. 'And he's in trouble!'

A loud, buzzing, clicking noise echoed round the trees.

'What's that?' panted Jamie, picking up speed.

'It sounds like a hundred electric drills!' exclaimed Tom, as they headed towards their little friend's frightened cries.

They scooted round a large boulder and found themselves in a clearing.

'There he is!' cried Jamie.

GRUUUUUNK!

Wanna was standing on a rock, clutching a gingko in his front claws. His eyes were wide with terror. All around him was a seething black horde of insects.

'Giant cockroaches!' Tom gawped in horror at the thousands of shiny creatures, each as long as the boys' hands.

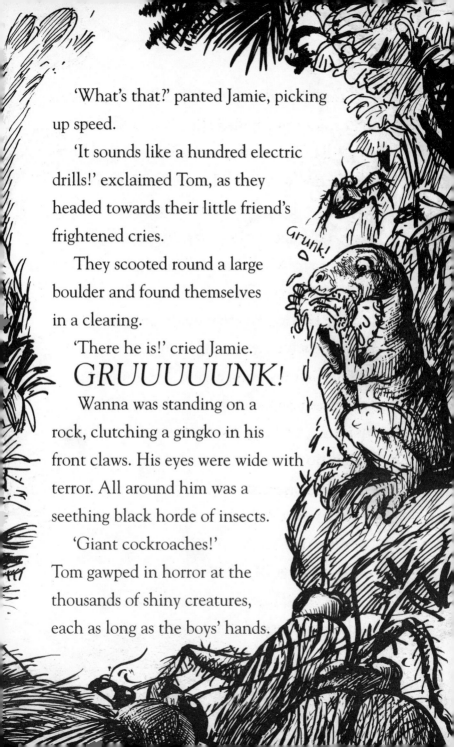

Grunk!

'And they're after Wanna's gingko!'
Jamie shuddered. 'They're
like armoured tanks—and
check out those pincers
and hairy legs.'

'We've certainly found
our giant insects,' said
Tom grimly.

The beetle-like creatures were jostling and
butting each other, trying to be first to reach
Wanna's stinky orange fruit. Their antennae
twitched and frothy slime oozed from their
mouths. One began to crawl up Wanna's leg.
The little dinosaur squealed and shook it off,
whipping about to keep the creatures at bay.

'We've arrived just in time,' Jamie shouted
over the hum of the hungry insects. 'Don't
worry, Wanna! We'll rescue you.'

'We could lure them away with gingkoes,'
said Tom. He tried to reach some fruit on an

overhanging branch. 'No good. They're too high.'

'Then we'll have to scare them away somehow,' answered Jamie.

Tom thought hard. 'What are cockroaches frightened of?'

'Fire,' said Jamie decisively. 'Most creatures are scared of fire. And it'll be easy to light one with everything so dry.'

He snatched up two fallen branches that were lying at his feet, grabbed the magnifying glass and held it over them. A shaft of sunlight shone through the lens and made a dazzling pinpoint that seared into the withered brown leaves. Wisps of smoke curled

into the air, and the leaves burst into crackling flames.

Jamie handed a branch to Tom. 'Wanna, here we come!'

The boys advanced, waving their fiery torches at the ground. The cockroaches scattered frantically from the flames, moving away like a rippling black carpet.

'It's working!' yelled Tom. As the sea of insects parted, the trembling little dino took his chance.

He scrambled off his rock and charged towards the boys, the gingko flying from his claws. He scuttled behind Tom and peered out at his attackers.

'You're safe now!' Jamie told him, stroking his hard, domed head. 'We've seen enough giant insects, I think. Let's go home, or we'll end up in Dad's museum.'

Grunk!

Wanna was looking crossly at his fallen gingko.

A cockroach had snatched the fruit up in its pincers. The others immediately attacked it, and soon the shiny black bodies were writhing ferociously, slurping and snapping their jaws, each one trying to reach the tasty meal.

Suddenly the force of the fight threw
one of the cockroaches into the air. It spun
towards the boys. They ducked just in
time and it smashed against a tree trunk,
splattering them both in sticky yellow goo.

'Gross!' exclaimed Jamie, wiping
his eyes. 'Dead bug slime!'

'There's worse to come,' warned
Tom. 'They're coming for us!'

Having finished the gingko,
the insects swarmed towards the
boys and Wanna.

'They must think he's got
more food,' said Jamie, trying to
shield their little friend from view.

They edged away but the advancing army
soon reached their feet.

'Ow!' yelped Jamie, clutching his ankle.
'I've been bitten!'

He waved his burning torch at the
cockroaches and they reared back—but only for
a second. Then they were on the move again.

Wanna gave a whimpering *grunk*.

Tom's eyes were wide with alarm. 'Let's get
out of here!'

CHAPTER 3

Jamie, Tom, and Wanna crashed through
the undergrowth. The forest was thicker
here, lit only where the sun filtered through
the trees. The buzzing, clicking sounds of the
cockroaches followed them as they ran.

'Much wetter . . . underfoot . . . than last
time,' puffed Jamie.

They jumped over puddles of water and
pushed through the boggy foliage. At last they
burst into a clearing with a huge pond in the
middle. The blue water was sparkling.

'Can you hear the cockroaches?' asked Tom, slowing at last.

'No.' Jamie stopped and took deep gulps of air. 'We're safe—for the moment.'

'Let's get rid of these,' said Tom, throwing his flaming torch into the pond. The leaves fizzled as the fire went out.

'Those beasts were nothing like the cockroaches back home,' said Jamie, tapping the keys on his Fossil Finder. The screen flashed and he read the entry aloud. 'They've got a funny name,' he said. 'You pronounce it ap-thor-oh-blat-in-a.' He read on. 'Apthoroblattina are the ancestors of today's cockroaches. It says they're fearsome predators, so it's lucky we found Wanna when we did or he'd have been on their menu.'

APTHOROBLATTINA

SEARCH: PERMIAN COCKROACH

A corner of the pond
was bubbling. Tom waved
his hands in front of his face
to try to clear the smell of
rotten eggs. 'Phew-wee,' he
said. 'I reckon it's getting
smellier. The extinction
event could happen at any
moment. Which way's our cave?'

Jamie pointed through the trees. 'We need
to head that way. Let's keep Wanna close to
us. The sooner we're back home and he's in
the Cretaceous again, the better.'

The boys rounded the edge of the pond, the
gloopy mud sucking on their trainers. Wanna
hopped over the puddles of steaming water.

Tom caught Jamie's arm. 'Can you hear that?' he whispered.

Jamie listened. A deep droning sound was coming from the centre of the pool.

'That's not cockroaches,' he whispered back. 'More like one of those old-fashioned aeroplanes that fly over the cove.'

The droning grew louder and a flat leaf in the water quivered as a large winged insect took to the air.

'There's your plane!' laughed Tom. He pretended to speak into an imaginary microphone. 'And here we see a prehistoric dragonfly. It's longer than my arm and the sunlight is catching its delicate blue-green wings. Now Professor Morgan will give us its proper name.'

Tom held the imaginary mike under Jamie's nose.

Jamie grinned and tapped 'PERMIAN

DRAGONFLY' into the Fossil Finder. 'It's called Odonata,' he reported in a deep, serious voice. 'It's the oldest winged creature ever discovered.'

'Awesome!' gasped Tom.

The boys watched in amazement as the huge glistening dragonfly skimmed the surface of the water. Humming low, it zigzagged across the pond before settling on a branch.

'At least this insect doesn't want to eat us,' said Jamie, laughing. As they turned to leave, the shimmering creature took off and hovered over them.

'It's a bit close,' said Tom.

'Too close,' yelled Jamie, jumping aside as the dragonfly dived at his head. It zoomed past him but turned and swooped again, droning loudly, wings scything the air.

Jamie swatted at the creature and it swerved away. 'What's the matter with it?' he gasped.

'I don't know,' said Tom. 'But here come reinforcements.'

Two more dragonflies, as big as the first, were whizzing towards them and others appeared from the undergrowth. The air darkened with the swelling mass of droning insects.

'It's a swarm,' cried Jamie. 'I spoke too soon—they *do* want to eat us.'

The dragonflies dived at the boys, slapping their faces and arms with their wings.

Grunk!

Wanna cowered behind Tom's legs in fright.

A huge dragonfly landed on Jamie's shoulder. 'Wow, it's heavy!' he groaned, trying to shake it free. It clung on, biting at his T-shirt. 'And it's got strong jaws.'

'It's not us they're after,' Tom told him, waving his arms to ward off the attack. 'It's our cockroach goo.'

Jamie gave a great swipe and sent the dragonfly spinning. 'Let's clean it off, then.'

Grunk!

He was about to jump in the pool when
the swarm descended on them. For a moment
the boys could hardly see for the cloud of
flying insects that surrounded them.

'There's only one thing to do,' Jamie
yelled. 'Run!'

CHAPTER 4

SEARCH:

Jamie and Tom hurtled off through the trees,
jumping the ferns and low boulders in their
path. Wanna sped ahead.

'The dragonflies are still coming!' panted
Jamie. 'We can't outrun them.'

'Look!' gasped Tom. He pointed to the top
of the volcano, which was just visible above
the trees. 'Our cave's over there. We'll soon
be home.'

'Where the insects are normal-size!'
agreed Jamie.

'And the world isn't about to blow up,' added Tom.

They ran through the last of the trees and onto the plain.

'We've come out in a different place,' puffed Jamie, worried. 'I can't see our cave.'

'The jungle's way over there in the distance,' said Tom. 'So we must be further east. They'll catch us up before we reach our cave.'

The heavy humming sound was battering their ears now. 'We've got to try!' yelled Jamie.

Whoosh!

The boys and Wanna tore across the plain, dodging the spurting geysers of red-hot lava.

Jamie checked over his shoulder. A blur of fast-moving wings was right behind them.

'Dive-bombers!' he shouted. 'Get down!'

They threw themselves to the ground. The streamlined insect air force whizzed over their heads.

'Now we know what a mouse feels like when a hawk's after it!' gasped Tom. 'We need to get under cover.'

Jamie looked frantically up the slope. 'I can see an opening,' he called. 'Let's shelter there and head for the cave when they're gone.'

'Sounds good to me,' Tom called back. 'Wanna and I are right behind you!'

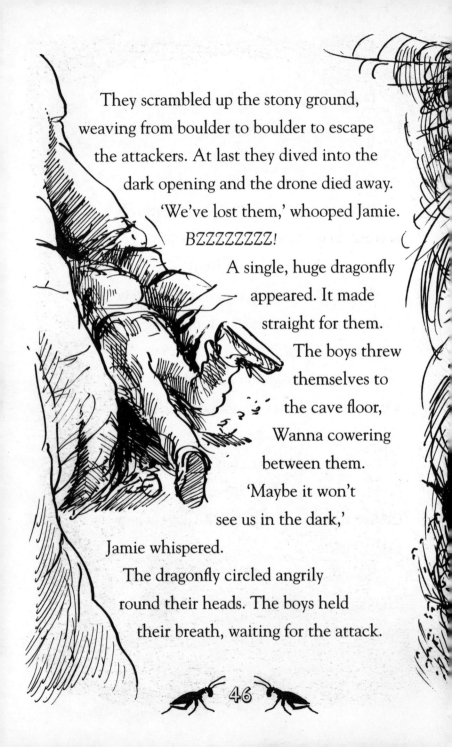

They scrambled up the stony ground,
weaving from boulder to boulder to escape
the attackers. At last they dived into the
dark opening and the drone died away.
'We've lost them,' whooped Jamie.
BZZZZZZZZ!

A single, huge dragonfly
appeared. It made
straight for them.

The boys threw
themselves to
the cave floor,
Wanna cowering
between them.

'Maybe it won't
see us in the dark,'
Jamie whispered.

The dragonfly circled angrily
round their heads. The boys held
their breath, waiting for the attack.

46

But nothing happened.

The sound of its wings stopped
for a second, then it burst into a
frantic buzzing.

Jamie peered up at the giant insect. It
seemed to be hovering in mid-air, its
wings twitching.

'It must be getting ready to attack!' he
exclaimed. He lurched back in alarm and
crashed into Tom and Wanna. They
all went sprawling over the
cave floor.

Jamie felt himself sink into a pile of
something soft that clutched at his arms and
legs, bringing him to a sudden halt. He tried
to get up but he couldn't move. Sticky webs
as thick as his finger were wrapped round him.
He pulled hard but they held him tight.

'I'm trapped!' he yelled.

'Me too,' Tom called through the dark
shadows of the cave.

Grunk!

'And so's Wanna!'
groaned Jamie.

He looked frantically
around and soon wished
he hadn't.

'We're in a spider's
web,' he gasped,
pointing up at the
cocoons of white
sticky net that

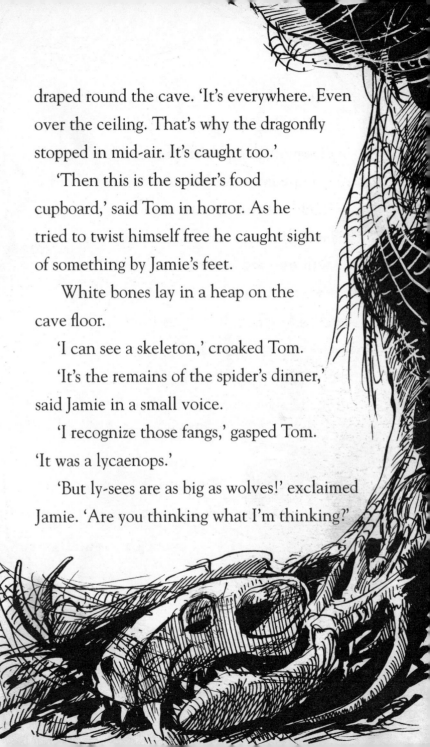

draped round the cave. 'It's everywhere. Even
over the ceiling. That's why the dragonfly
stopped in mid-air. It's caught too.'

'Then this is the spider's food
cupboard,' said Tom in horror. As he
tried to twist himself free he caught sight
of something by Jamie's feet.

White bones lay in a heap on the
cave floor.

'I can see a skeleton,' croaked Tom.

'It's the remains of the spider's dinner,'
said Jamie in a small voice.

'I recognize those fangs,' gasped Tom.
'It was a lycaenops.'

'But ly-sees are as big as wolves!' exclaimed
Jamie. 'Are you thinking what I'm thinking?'

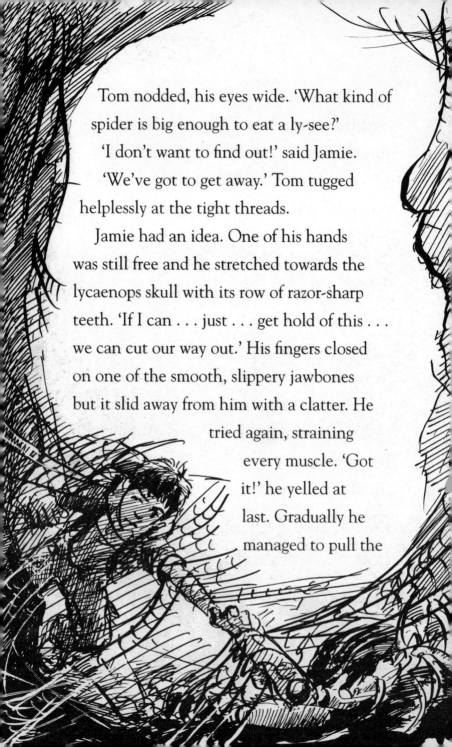

Tom nodded, his eyes wide. 'What kind of spider is big enough to eat a ly-see?'

'I don't want to find out!' said Jamie.

'We've got to get away.' Tom tugged helplessly at the tight threads.

Jamie had an idea. One of his hands was still free and he stretched towards the lycaenops skull with its row of razor-sharp teeth. 'If I can . . . just . . . get hold of this . . . we can cut our way out.' His fingers closed on one of the smooth, slippery jawbones but it slid away from him with a clatter. He tried again, straining every muscle. 'Got it!' he yelled at last. Gradually he managed to pull the jawbone towards him. Holding it tightly, he used the sharp fangs to begin sawing through the strands of web that held his other arm. 'Once I'm free, I'll get you and Wanna out.'

'Good plan!' said Tom.

Grunk!

'You'll have to be patient, Wanna,' Jamie called as he freed his arm and hacked away the strands around his legs. 'This web's mega strong!'

Grunk! Grunk!

The little dinosaur was thrashing about in terror and staring into a dark corner.

'Jamie!' yelled Tom. 'Over there.'

Tom was staring
hard into the corner
too. In the deep
shadows,

something was
moving slowly across
the web. Jamie could make

out two antennae, eight long legs, and a huge, crablike body.

He didn't need the Fossil Finder to tell him what it was. It might be a lot bigger than its modern-day counterpart, but he knew a spider when he saw one.

'It's massive!' breathed Tom. 'As big as a dog.'

'Bigger,' muttered Jamie. 'But if we're dead still it might not see us.'

'And if it does, we're just dead,'
added Tom.

The boys watched in frozen horror as the
spider crawled across the ceiling towards the
trapped dragonfly, its hairy legs feeling their
way along the web.

'If the spider fills itself up, it won't have
room for any more food,' whispered Jamie.
'We'll have time to escape.'

The spider reached its prey and hung over
it for a moment. Then its sting struck out.
The dragonfly jerked once and was still.

Crawling all over its paralysed victim,
the giant predator began spinning it into

a cocoon. Suddenly it stopped, antennae
waving in the air. It turned and began to head
in Tom's direction.

'I reckon it's picked up the scent of
cockroach goo!' whispered Tom. 'Just like the
dragonflies did.'

'And that means one thing,' Jamie
whispered back. 'We're a spider snack!'

CHAPTER 5

SEARCH:

ABCDEFGHIJKLMN
PQRSTUVWXYZ

Jamie frantically pulled his legs free. 'I'm out!'
he exclaimed.

The spider was coming straight for Tom,
making its way down the web.

Jamie ran over to release him, sawing at
the web with the ly-see jawbone. 'Nearly
there,' he cried, tearing the last strands of web
from Tom's trainers.

Tom snatched up another jawbone and
held it like a knife. 'Now for Wanna!'

Grunk! Grunk! GRUNK!

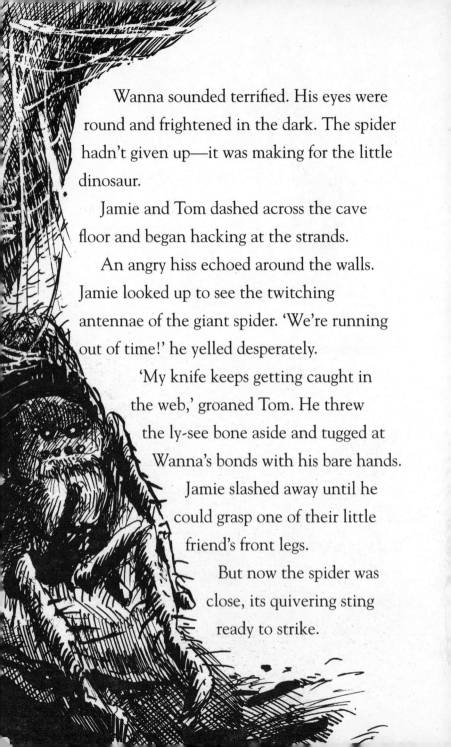

Wanna sounded terrified. His eyes were round and frightened in the dark. The spider hadn't given up—it was making for the little dinosaur.

Jamie and Tom dashed across the cave floor and began hacking at the strands.

An angry hiss echoed around the walls. Jamie looked up to see the twitching antennae of the giant spider. 'We're running out of time!' he yelled desperately.

'My knife keeps getting caught in the web,' groaned Tom. He threw the ly-see bone aside and tugged at Wanna's bonds with his bare hands.

Jamie slashed away until he could grasp one of their little friend's front legs.

But now the spider was close, its quivering sting ready to strike.

'Pull!' bellowed Jamie.

Tom didn't need to be told twice.
Together, he and Jamie yanked the web as
hard as they could. Just as the spider's deadly
sting flashed down, they tore Wanna free. But
the danger wasn't over. As they scrambled
towards the cave entrance a scuttling noise
from behind let them know that the spider
was still in pursuit.

They threw themselves out of the cave, blinking in the sudden, dazzling sunlight.

Tom skidded to a halt.

'Move!' gasped Jamie, cannoning into him. 'We've got to get to our cave.'

'We can't,' whispered Tom. 'Look who's turned up!'

Jamie heard a familiar sound.

GRRRRHHHH!

A bear-like creature with matted fur and razor-sharp teeth was standing in their way. It pawed at the red dust and lowered its head, ready to charge. The low rumbling in its throat was growing louder.

Wanna clung to them, giving tiny, terrified *grunks*.

'The inostie!' muttered Jamie out of the corner of his mouth. 'Might have known it would turn up.'

'We're trapped,' Tom muttered back.

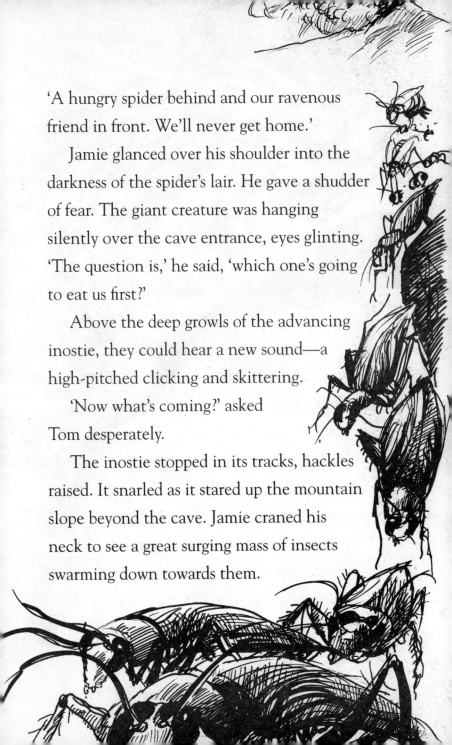

'A hungry spider behind and our ravenous friend in front. We'll never get home.'

Jamie glanced over his shoulder into the darkness of the spider's lair. He gave a shudder of fear. The giant creature was hanging silently over the cave entrance, eyes glinting. 'The question is,' he said, 'which one's going to eat us first?'

Above the deep growls of the advancing inostie, they could hear a new sound—a high-pitched clicking and skittering.

'Now what's coming?' asked Tom desperately.

The inostie stopped in its tracks, hackles raised. It snarled as it stared up the mountain slope beyond the cave. Jamie craned his neck to see a great surging mass of insects swarming down towards them.

'Cockroaches again,'
gasped Jamie. 'Coming
our way.'

'But they're not after us,' said
Tom, gulping. 'Look what they're
running from.'

Behind the sea of scuttling insects,
a gigantic plume of fiery lava was
shooting into the air. It hit the ground and
tumbled down the mountain in a deadly

river, sweeping away rocks and trees in its
path. Soon the insects at the head of the
charge were racing past the boys' feet. Tom
glanced back. The spider was vanishing into
the cave.

He nudged Jamie. 'One enemy down, one
to go.'

'And there goes the other one!'
exclaimed Jamie.

The terrified inostie was backing
away from the approaching insects.

But too late—they surged under its feet and carried it away on their backs.

'Awesome! We're safe.' Tom could feel his heartbeat settling, until a cry from Jamie sent it racing again.

'Look where the lava's heading!' he yelled. 'Right for *our* cave. We won't be able to get home.'

Tom gasped. 'That means it won't just be the end of the Permian—it'll be the end of us too!'

CHAPTER 6

'I've got an idea,' exclaimed Jamie. 'But you're not going to like it.'

'I'm listening,' said Tom urgently. 'That lava's coming fast, so any idea's good.'

'Let's hitch a lift!' explained Jamie. 'The cockroaches are going our way, and if they can carry an inostrancevia they'll have no problem with our puny weight as long as we lie flat.'

Tom punched the air. 'Let's do it!'

They lay on their stomachs and wriggled on to the moving cockroach carpet.

'Copy us, Wanna,' coaxed Jamie, pulling the trembling little dinosaur down to join them. The insects didn't seem to notice the boys and Wanna as they pelted away from the hot river of lava.

'This goo we're covered in is useful at last,' cried Tom. 'They think we're one of them.'

The cockroaches sped along, clicking loudly. It was a bumpy ride and the boys were jolted from side to side, but they covered the ground at tremendous speed. Soon the spider's cave was left far behind.

Jamie let out a whoop. 'Dinosaur Cove— here we come!'

'I think we're just in time,' added Tom.

POP! POP! POP!

All around them, jets of lava shot up into the sky like fountains of fire. They cast a weird, red glow over the boys' faces. Black clouds of smoke rolled over the scorched landscape. Wanna spluttered and Jamie wiped his eyes, which were streaming in the thick, putrid air. On the horizon, a herd of creatures with fan-like sails on their backs were charging out of a burning copse of trees.

'Dimetrodon,' said Jamie, remembering their first visit to the Permian era. 'I hope they manage to find shelter.'

POP!

There was a sudden noise behind him and he twisted round to look over his shoulder.

POP! POP!

'Gross!' he exclaimed. 'The lava's reached the cockroaches at the back of the pack. They're exploding like popcorn.'

'Then it's going to reach us soon,' gasped Tom. 'We've got to get off this travelator.'

'Our cave's just ahead!' cried Jamie. 'Get ready to roll.'

The two boys threw themselves sideways, tumbling off their shiny black carpet and onto the stony ground.

Grunk!

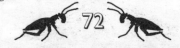

Wanna landed on top of them. In a flash, he jumped up and disappeared inside the cave. Tom launched himself after him and began to climb down.

Jamie took one last look at the Permian. It was ablaze with red flame. The wave of lava was close now and the sound of popping cockroach bodies was like gunfire.

'It's now or never!' he yelled and

SSSSSSS!

dived for the opening in the rock.

Tom and Wanna were waiting
for him at the bottom. Wanna greeted
him with huge, raspy licks.

SSSSSSSS!

The hot red river rushed past the cave
entrance. Some of it gushed down into the
cave itself, spattering in hot pools on the rock.

'Hurry!' yelled Tom.

They ran to the dinosaur footprints in the
sand. Wanna galloped off towards the back
of the cave, then turned and looked back at
the boys.

Grunk!

'I think he's saying goodbye,' Jamie said.

'Bye, Wanna!' both boys called.

The little dino gave a final grunk and
disappeared into the darkness.

'He'll be back home in the Cretaceous
now,' said Tom.

'And we're almost home too,' said Jamie in relief.

The boys scrambled out of the smugglers' cave and stood in the gentle sunshine of Dinosaur Cove.

'I'm glad to see the insect goo has turned to dust,' said Tom, brushing at his T-shirt. 'That would have taken some explaining.'

'No one would believe that just one cockroach could make so much mess,' said Jamie as they ran across the beach towards the lighthouse. 'But of course they wouldn't know how big it was.'

They reached the tree and knelt down to inspect the sheet. There were a few insects still on it. Tom pointed to a spider scuttling about.

'That reminds me,' he said with a grin. 'What was that beastie called back there in the cave?'

Jamie took out his Fossil Finder and tapped in *PERMIAN SPIDER*. 'It's called a—perm-ar-ak-nee,' he read. 'At least we haven't got any permarachnes here.'

Tom watched a beetle crawl onto his finger. 'This has got the same exoskeleton as the Permian cockroaches,' he said. 'So although there was that big extinction two hundred and fifty million years ago, some insects did make it through.'

'I'm pleased they did,' said Jamie, inspecting the shiny back of the beetle. 'But I'm even more pleased they got smaller!'

DINOSAUR WORLD

BOYS' ROUTE

Mountains

Volcano

Underground cave

Jungle

Desert

Permian Sea

Pools of water

Swamp

Forest

Permian Sea

77

GLOSSARY

Apthoroblattina (ap-thor-oh-blat-in-a) – an extinct bug. It was like a modern-day cockroach, but much bigger.

Cretaceous (cret-ay-shus) – from about 65 to 150 million years ago, this time period was home to the widest variety of dinosaur and insect life of any period. Birds replaced winged dinosaurs, while in the sea, sharks and rays multiplied.

Dimetrodon (dy-mee-tr-oh-don) – a sail-backed, mammal-like reptile.

Exoskeleton (ex-oh-skel-e-ton) – a skeleton that is on the outside of a creature's body, rather than inside. Insects have exoskeletons.

Gingko (gink-oh) – a tree native to China called a 'living fossil' because fossils of it have been found dating back millions of years, yet they are still around today. Also known as the stink bomb tree because of its smelly apricot-like fruit.

Hydrogen sulphide (hy-dro-jen sul-fy-d) – a gas that cannot be seen, but it is very poisonous and easily catches fire. It smells like rotten eggs.

Inostrancevia (in-os-tran-see-vee-ah) – a large, predatory mammal-like reptile.

Lycaenops (ly-see-nops) – a wolf-like reptile which hunted in packs. Its name means 'wolf face'.

Odonata (oh-don-a-ta) – a giant prehistoric dragonfly. It is the oldest creature with wings to have been discovered.

Permarachne (perm-ar-ak-nee) – a primitive spider. It was larger than modern-day spiders and could spin gigantic webs.

Permian (per-mee-an) – the Permian period lasted from 290 to 248 million years ago. During this time the supercontinent Pangaea was formed and non-dinosaur reptiles roamed the earth.

Trilobite (try-loh-byt) – an extinct marine animal that had an exoskeleton divided into three parts.

Wannanosaurus (wah-nan-oh-sor-us) – a dinosaur that only ate plants and used its hard, flat skull to defend itself. Named after the place it was discovered: Wannano in China.